Picture This

Norah McClintock

orca soundings

ORCA BOOK PUBLISHERS

Library and Archives Canada Cataloguing in Publication

McClintock, Norah
Picture this / written by Norah McClintock.

(Orca soundings)
ISBN 978-1-55469-139-5 (bound).--ISBN 978-1-55469-138-8 (pbk.)

I. Title. II. Series: Orca soundings

PS8575.C62P52 2009   jC813'.54   C2009-902579-5

Summary: Ethan has a secret that someone is willing to kill for.

First published in the United States, 2009
Library of Congress Control Number: 2009927572

Orca Book Publishers gratefully acknowledges the support for
its publishing programs provided by the following agencies: the
Government of Canada through the Book Publishing Industry
Development Program and the Canada Council for the Arts, and the
Province of British Columbia through the BC Arts Council and
the Book Publishing Tax Credit.

Cover design by Teresa Bubela
Cover photography by Getty Images

ORCA BOOK PUBLISHERS   ORCA BOOK PUBLISHERS
PO Box 5626, STN. B   PO Box 468
VICTORIA, BC CANADA   CUSTER, WA USA
V8R 6S4   98240-0468

www.orcabook.com
Printed and bound in Canada.
Printed on 100% PCW recycled paper.
12 11 10 09 • 4 3 2 1

To P.S. and those nice bright colors.

Chapter One

It was my own stupid fault, just like everything else in my messed-up life.

"It's all about choices," Deacon, my youth worker, always used to say. "There are good choices and bad choices, and each one leads to more choices."

Okay, so it was a bad choice to decide to take a shortcut through a dark alley. Not that I expect anyone to believe me, but I actually thought about it before I did it. And I chose to take the shortcut anyway because (a) I'm a guy, not a girl, so it wasn't like I had to be afraid that some crazy guy would attack me and drag me behind some bushes, and (b) I was in a hurry to get home before my foster mom started to worry. So I ducked into the alley.

I was exactly halfway down it, kicking a stone ahead of me and enjoying the rattling sound it made as it skipped across the broken asphalt ahead of me, when a guy came up behind me, stuck something hard into my back and offered me another choice: Hand over my backpack *or else*.

I stuck my hands up in the air and turned around slowly. Maybe you wouldn't have done that. Maybe you would have just dropped that backpack without a second's hesitation. But I wanted to know who I was dealing with—a guy who was pretending to have a gun shoved in my back or a guy who actually had a gun shoved in my back.

The guy was holding what looked like a real gun. He was wearing a balaclava, you know, one of those hood-like things that guys pull over their heads when they're up to no good. All I could see were his eyes, which were hard and cold, and his mouth, which was small and mean.

"Hand it over," he said when I didn't immediately do what he wanted.

"You've got the wrong guy," I said.

I know. You probably would have kept your mouth shut. But, really, he did have the wrong guy. I wasn't some rich kid. There was no wallet bulging with cash and credit cards in my backpack. There was no bank card that he could grab or force me to use. There was nothing in there worth stealing except maybe my camera, and even that wasn't worth much to anyone except me. There was no way I wanted to hand it over to someone who would either toss it or sell it for five or ten bucks.

"Don't make me say it again," the guy said. He raised the gun and pointed it at my head.

I stared at the barrel. Up close, it looked as big as a cannon. My legs were shaking. I looked straight into the guy's cold, hard eyes.

"Seriously," I said. "There's nothing in my backpack. I'm broke. I live with foster parents. And they only took me in because of the money the government pays them."

Only part of that was true. The Ashdales probably would have taken me in even if they didn't get paid. It wasn't about the money for them. They were foster parents because they wanted to make a difference in the lives of kids like me. They were strict, but they were nice.

"This is your last chance," the guy said.

I know what you're thinking: What's the matter with you, Ethan? Give the man the backpack before he hurts you. But you're not me. You don't understand how much that camera meant to me. You don't understand what it would have been like to let some nut job with a gun grab it and either junk it or sell it for cash, probably so he could get high.

I stared at that gun again. It looked real enough, but, come on, the guy was mugging *me*. What were the chances that anyone would come at a kid with a loaded gun just to get a backpack that might contain a few dollars or a bank card or maybe an iPod? You have to be hard up to do something like that. Either that or you have to be totally out of it, some kind of crazy or drugged-up junkie. Idiots like that don't carry real guns. They can't afford to. It had to be a fake.

I glanced at the stone I had been fooling around with—it was a couple of inches from my foot—and made my choice.

I lowered my hands slowly to my shoulders, watching the guy the whole time to make sure he understood that I was moving them toward the straps of my backpack. I saw the same satisfaction in his eyes that I had seen in the eyes of dozens of bullies over the years, the pure joy they always experience when they succeed in forcing someone to give them what they want.

Then quickly, trying not to think about what I was doing, I kicked the stone as hard as I could. It ricocheted off a dumpster, startling the guy. When he turned his head to see what had happened, I swung my backpack hard at the hand holding the gun. The gun clattered to the ground, and I kicked it as hard as I could in the other direction. Then I sprinted down the alley. I was almost at the other end when I heard a shot. I felt sick inside. The gun was loaded after all.

I powered on the speed. I never once looked behind me—it would only have slowed me down. I zigzagged through alleys and up and down streets. I ran until I was sure my lungs would explode.

When I reached my street, I slowed down. No one was following me. I stopped, gasping and panting, and looked around again. Still I saw no one. My breathing returned to normal. I ran up the front walk, opened the door and was greeted by the smell of Mrs. Ashdale's meat loaf. Home sweet home, I thought. I was safe. Nothing would happen to me here.

Chapter Two

"Perfect timing," Mrs. Ashdale said when she saw me. She pulled the meat loaf out of the oven. "Set the table, would you, Ethan? And then call the others."

The others were Alan, who was eleven and who had been seized by child welfare because his mother, a meth-head, had been neglecting him, and Tricia, nine, whose dad had abandoned her after her mother died. Alan had been with the Ashdales for nearly four years. He was okay. Tricia was new. She cried a lot and had major temper tantrums. I had been with the Ashdales for almost a year, ever since my last foster mother had a heart attack and couldn't handle kids anymore. I mainly got along okay with Mrs. Ashdale, who stayed home, and Mr. Ashdale, who was in charge of a couple of recreation centers in the city. They didn't have kids of their own. I'm not sure why.

"Bill won't be home for supper," Mrs. Ashdale said as I opened the drawer to get the cutlery. "It's just the four of us."

I set the table and called Alan and Tricia. By the time they came downstairs, Mrs. Ashdale had set out the food. We all knew better than to dig in. We waited until Mrs. Ashdale said grace. Then we passed our plates so that she could serve out thick slabs of meat loaf, big scoops of fluffy mashed potatoes and fresh green peas. It sounds pretty ordinary, but it tasted great. Mrs. Ashdale was a good cook.

"So, how was everyone's day?" she said when we all had full plates. "Alan?"

Both Alan and Tricia were going to day camp for the month. Alan went to a sports camp at one of the rec centers. Tricia went to a nature camp on the island.

"We played soccer against another camp," Alan said. "I scored three goals." Alan was a soccer fanatic. He knew which teams and which players were the best in the world. He wanted to play professional soccer. He might even do it too. He was good for a little kid, and he practiced every chance he got. Sometimes Mr. Ashdale called him Beckham, and Alan looked like he would burst with pride.

Mrs. Ashdale smiled at him. "That's great, Alan," she said. "How about you, Tricia?"

"We counted frogs," Tricia said in a small, whispery voice. "I found some that no one else saw. My counselor said I have sharp eyes." I thought that was kind of funny, because she didn't look up from her plate even once. She was quiet when she wasn't freaking out.

"It's good to be observant," Mrs. Ashdale said. "With your interest in nature and your sharp eyes, you could grow up to be a biologist. Or a botanist. Or a zoologist." She explained what each of those things was and why they were all important. Tricia kept her eyes on her plate, but Mrs. Ashdale didn't let that bother her.

"What about you, Ethan?" Mrs. Ashdale said to me. "How's the project going?"

I was too old for baby camps, so my youth worker suggested that I take part in a special program for kids like me, which is to say, at-risk kids. Kids who have been in trouble. Kids who need to turn their lives around before it's too late. The program was called Picture This. It taught kids the basics of photography and gave them special projects to work on, which we were supposed to talk about regularly in a group. The idea was to really look at the world around us and to try to capture it with our cameras.

We spent the first couple of weeks learning how cameras work and experimenting with composition, framing and photo editing on the computer. Now we were working on our own projects.

"So far, so good, I guess," I said. "But I'm probably going to have to go back for more pictures. I want to see if I can get closer this time."

We were supposed to pick a theme and illustrate it with photographs. I picked freedom. I wanted to show that it isn't possible for a person to be completely free, because there is always something—usually more than one thing—that puts serious limits on freedom. To do that, I was documenting a couple of hawks I'd discovered in the woods north of the city one time when Mr. Ashdale took me hiking. Hawks look like they're totally free, especially when they're soaring high against a clear blue sky. They're birds of prey, powerful birds that take whatever they want from nature. They're like a lot of guys I used to know. They look and act like kings. But they aren't completely free. Not only was the hawks' habitat endangered, but so was the habitat of their prey, thanks to people. It was getting harder and harder for those kings of the sky to get what they wanted. And it was going to get even worse, just like things almost always turned bad for the guys I used to know, guys in gangs who thought they could do whatever they wanted, but who ended up either dead or in prison.

My project was going really well. I was proud of what I'd done so far. All my pictures were in the digital camera that the Ashdales had bought me for my birthday back in April. That's why I didn't want to hand it over to the guy in the alley. I didn't tell Mrs. Ashdale about what had happened. I didn't want her to worry.

"I'll probably head up there again tomorrow, if that's okay with you," I said. "I have a note from DeVon." DeVon Loomis was in charge of the Picture This program. I'd asked him to write the note so that Mrs. Ashdale wouldn't think I was trying to duck the program for a day. I dug it out of my pocket and handed it to her. She didn't read it. She just smiled and set it next to her plate.

"I'd love to see what you've done so far," she said. "Maybe you could show me after we clean up the kitchen."

"Sure," I said. If I had to name only one thing that I liked about the Ashdales, it was that they were really interested in what I was doing. It wasn't a put-on. They actually listened when I told them how my day had been or what assignments I was working on for school. So I was more than happy to get out my camera later that evening and show Mrs. Ashdale my pictures. She exclaimed over the ones that I thought were the best and asked a lot of questions.

"Who's that?" she said, pointing to the camera display screen. I squinted at it.

"Just some guy," I said. He was a middle-aged man, and he was leaning on a shovel. He was in the bottom corner of two of my pictures. "I need those shots," I said. "I figured I could edit him out."

"You can do that?" Mrs. Ashdale said. She sounded surprised.

"With the software they have at the youth center, you can do anything," I told her.

I had a few more pictures to show her, but we were interrupted by a crash and a shout from Alan: "Tricia's breaking things again!"

Mrs. Ashdale sighed.

"If you haven't already, you should make backup copies of your pictures, Ethan," she said. She sounded like DeVon. He was always bugging me to back up my work.

"I will," I said. "After I get the last few shots I need."

She ran up the stairs to deal with Tricia. I looked through my pictures again and made a list in my head of what I needed to complete my project. It'll be easy, I thought.

Chapter Three

I got up early the next morning and made myself a couple of peanut butter sandwiches. I put them in my backpack along with an orange and a bottle of water. Then I headed out. I had to take two city buses and then transfer to a completely different bus line to get where I was going. It was like traveling to another country.

The bus driver let me off at the side of a two-lane highway. I darted across it and walked against traffic to a graveled side road. Fifteen minutes later, I left the graveled road for a path that led into the forest where Mr. Ashdale had taken me hiking that time.

It was cool and peaceful in among the trees. Everything smelled like pine and wildflowers, and I heard the babble of a stream running, hidden through the trees. Every now and then a chipmunk scurried across the trail ahead of me, and I heard the call of birds overhead. I wished I could tell what kind of birds they were just from the way they sounded, but I couldn't. I had to see them, and even then I only knew the basic ones: robins and blue jays, pigeons and seagulls, eagles and owls. And, of course, hawks.

I pulled out the map Mr. Ashdale had given me and that I had marked as best as I could so that I would remember where

I had been. I used it to guide me deep into the woods where I had found my two hawks. They weren't in their nest, so I settled down to wait for them.

Quiet and patience were good things when you were looking for birds, Mr. Ashdale had told me. Anyone from my old neighborhood, the one where I used to live before I was put into foster care, would tell you that I am not a quiet or patient person. Normally I wasn't. But there was something about being in the woods when there was no one else around that made me feel calm and peaceful. And there was something about scanning the treetops through the lens of a camera or a pair of binoculars that made me pay close attention to what I was looking at. An hour passed before I knew it, and I wasn't the least bit impatient or antsy for something to happen.

I took out one of my sandwiches and ate it between peeks through my binoculars. I peeled my orange and ate that too. I was about to start on my second sandwich when I saw my two hawks soaring high in the sky, doing a slow, wheeling, swooping dance up there against the clear, bright blue before finally setting their wings to sail for home.

I got a couple of good shots. Then, once they were nested, I crept up to the bottom of their tree and pointed my camera directly up. I could barely see their nest from way down below. I took a picture. Then I extended my telephoto lens halfway so I could make out the clump of twigs and leaves and who-knew-what-else the two birds had glued together to make a home. I took another picture. Finally I extended my lens the whole way, for as close-up a shot as I could get. I took that picture too. I returned to where I had been sitting, unwrapped my second sandwich and ate while I waited for the hawks to go hunting.

It was midafternoon, and I hadn't done much except sit, watch and wait. But I finally got what I needed. I checked to make sure I had picked up all my garbage—like Mr. Ashdale had taught me—and I headed back to the highway to catch a bus home.

I was still in a pretty mellow mood by the time I got back to the city. I couldn't wait to show Mrs. Ashdale my new pictures. I knew she would appreciate them. So I was swinging along, humming to myself, when I got to the end of my street. That's when I saw the cop cars—two of them—pulled up to the curb in front of the Ashdales' house. In the old days, I would have been shaking all over, sure that they had come for me. But I hadn't done anything wrong since I'd been living with the Ashdales, so I knew I was in the clear. I ran up the street to see what had happened.

Mrs. Ashdale was standing on the front walk, talking to a cop in uniform. She nodded when she saw me, and the cop she was with turned. Just my luck. It was Officer Firelli. He'd busted me a few times over the years.

"Hello, Ethan," he said with a smirk on his face to tell me he remembered me and how messed up I used to be.

I ignored him.

"What happened?" I asked Mrs. Ashdale. "Are the kids okay?"

"They're fine," Mrs. Ashdale said. "I sent Meaghan to pick them up from the bus." Meaghan was my age. She lived down the street. "Someone broke into the house while I was out shopping," she said.

"Broke into the house? Did they take anything?"

"That's the weird thing," Mrs. Ashdale said. "I can't see that anything's missing. But they made a real mess of the place.

It's going to take forever to get everything put back where it belongs."

"Someone broke in and *didn't* take anything?" That didn't make sense. Then, just like that, my heart stopped. "They must have been in the house when you got home. You must have walked in on them." I could see it—some crack addicts were about to loot the place when they heard a key turn in the front door. "You could have been hurt, Mrs. Ashdale." And, boy, I would have hated for that to happen. I liked Mrs. Ashdale. She didn't deserve to have some crack addict attack her.

"*You* wouldn't know anything about what happened here today, would you, Ethan?" Officer Firelli said. He was in his late twenties and a real hardnose. I always had the feeling that he didn't like me.

"Me?" I said. "What do you mean?"

He shook his head as if he had asked me the easiest math question in the world and I was so dumb I couldn't even find the answer by counting on my fingers.

"Come on, Ethan," he said. "Are you going to pretend you didn't get that gang of yours to break into Mrs. Girardi's place when you were living there?"

I glanced at Mrs. Ashdale. My cheeks were burning. It was true what Officer Firelli had said. At first I'd hated being put in foster care, and I didn't try to hide it. The second week I was at Mrs. Girardi's, I got together with the guys I used to hang with. We broke the lock on the back door, tossed the place, took whatever cash we could find along with whatever we could sell, and took off.

A couple of the neighbors saw us. The only person they recognized was me, and there was no way I was going to give up my friends. But you know what happened? Mrs. Girardi refused to press charges. She just shrugged and said she supposed she and I were going to have to work on getting used to each other. Then she got started cleaning up the place.

I watched her for a few minutes, and then I pitched in. I felt awful when I saw her pick up a photograph album that had been thrown onto the floor. Some pictures had fallen out and someone had ripped them up. She looked sad as she held up the pieces, but she didn't say a word, which made me feel worse. Usually when I did something bad, I got yelled at or punished. But not that time. After that, Mrs. Girardi and I got along just fine—until she had her heart attack.

But I didn't know if Mrs. Ashdale knew about what had happened, and I didn't want to tell her. I was too embarrassed. So far I had done everything right at her house. I didn't want her to think I was still the kind of person I used to be.

"It's okay, Ethan," Mrs. Ashdale said in a quiet voice. "The past is the past, remember?"

That was what she and Mr. Ashdale had told me when I first came to live with them: the past is the past, and now is now. I'd thought, yeah, right. That's the kind of stuff adults always say. But saying something is one thing, meaning it is another. When I looked at Mrs. Ashdale standing there on the front walk, I knew she meant it.

"I had nothing to do with it," I said to Officer Firelli. "I wasn't even in town today."

"No?" He looked like he didn't believe me. Worse, he looked like he didn't want to believe me. "What about your gang? What are they up to?"

"How would I know?" I said.

Mrs. Ashdale gave me a warning look. I knew what that meant: keep your cool.

"I mean, I haven't seen any of those guys in almost a year," I said. "I don't hang out with them anymore."

"You sure about that, Ethan?" Officer Firelli said. His tone was so snotty that I wanted to punch him in the face. But I didn't. Instead I looked—really looked—at Mrs. Ashdale. She looked back at me. She looked deep into my eyes. And she nodded.

"I'm sure," I said. "If it's okay with you"—and even if it wasn't—"I'm going inside to start cleaning up."

Mrs. Ashdale squeezed my arm as I passed her. "I'll be right in," she said.

Mrs. Ashdale hadn't been kidding. The place was the biggest mess I had ever seen. Every drawer had been pulled out and emptied onto the floor. Every cupboard had been ransacked. Every bookshelf had been cleaned out. Mattresses, pillows, sheets and blankets had been tossed to the floor. The big calendar on the fridge where Mrs. Ashdale kept track of everyone's appointments and activities was lying on the kitchen floor.

"Are you sure nothing is missing?" I asked Mrs. Ashdale when she finally came inside.

"I guess we'll find out when we start putting everything back," she said.

We got to work. When Meaghan showed up with Alan and Tricia, they helped too. So did Mr. Ashdale when he got home. It took most of the night, but we finally got everything back where it belonged.

"There's nothing missing," Mrs. Ashdale said as she sank down onto the sofa.

"You must have interrupted them," I said.

"Either that or they were looking for something, Anna," Mr. Ashdale said.

"Like what?" Mrs. Ashdale said. "We don't have anything worth stealing, Bill."

It was true. The house was okay, and there was always plenty to eat. But the furniture was kind of beat-up, the TV was old, the DVD player one of those cheapies from a discount store and the computer was so ancient it couldn't even run half the software that we used at the youth center. You'd have to be nuts to think you could find anything worth stealing at the Ashdales' house.

At least, that's what I thought at the time.

Chapter Four

I had to force myself to choke down the pizza that Mr. Ashdale had ordered as a treat, to reward Alan and Tricia and me for working so hard to get the house back in order. I couldn't sleep that night either. I tossed and turned and looked enviously at Alan, who always seemed to fall into a deep sleep the moment his head hit the pillow. I felt terrible about having lied to Mrs. Ashdale.

When I got put into foster care, my social worker said it would be good for me. She said at the very minimum it would get me away from the kids I used to hang out with, kids who were gang-member wannabes. I was one of those kids too. If you were in a gang, you were part of something. You knew there was always someone who had your back. You were respected. You had a place, which was more than I could say about the dump I used to live in with my father, who, if you ask me, is a total lowlife. He got busted for being part of a car-theft ring, but not an important part, not the brains of the operation. Not even close. He was one of the guys who worked in a chop shop for cash. But he knew what he was doing. He knew those cars were stolen. The prosecutor knew that my dad knew. They tried to make a deal with him—plead guilty and you'll do a little time. Roll over and tell us everything you know, you'll get probation. My dad refused. He claimed he had no idea what was going on. So they gave him as much time as they could, and I went to live with Mrs. Girardi. I didn't want to be there. I hated that I had no say over where I lived. That's why I got together with my friends and we trashed the place. I wasn't mad at Mrs. Girardi. Mostly I was angry at my dad. That was the last time I saw *all* of my old friends together. But it wasn't the last time I saw *any* of them.

A couple of weeks ago, just before the end of school, I went back to Mrs. Girardi's neighborhood. She'd always been good to me, and I wanted to see how she was doing. I'm glad that I went too. She was so happy to see me. But it made me sad to think about it now. Mrs. Girardi was in pretty bad shape. She had one of those little tubes that poked up both her nostrils to give her oxygen, and there was a big container of oxygen beside the chair where she was sitting. She had lost a lot of weight, and her skin was a dusty gray color. When I lived with her, she was always bustling around. But when I went to visit her, she didn't get up even once. I felt sorry for her, and I promised to visit her again.

Then, on the way back to the Ashdales' house, I ran into Tilo, one of my old friends. Well, I *sort of* ran into him.

Tilo was racing down the street toward me, and no wonder. He was being chased by three guys. I recognized who they were—they were all members of the Nine-Eights, real tough guys who got their name from the address of the high-rise where the original members had lived. They were rivals of the gang I used to hang around with, even though I wasn't a member. Tilo ran right past me and ducked into an alley. He looked scared. I didn't even think about what I was doing—I pretended I didn't know him and, when the Nine-Eights ran by, I stuck out my foot and tripped the first guy. He fell flat on his face. The second guy didn't react fast enough, and he fell on the first guy. The third guy almost went down—but at the last minute, he jumped over his buddies and spun around to look at me. The fierce look on his face told me that he had changed targets. He didn't care about Tilo anymore. He wanted me.

I took off.

I didn't look back, but I heard feet pounding the cement behind me.

I raced for a main street. There would be a lot of people out there. I would be safer—maybe.

A hand hooked my shoulder. I tried to shake it off. A second hand hooked my other shoulder. Before I knew it, I had been jerked off my feet and was lying on my back on the sidewalk. The guy who had been chasing me threw himself onto me, but I twisted out of his way. He landed on the cement. I tried to get up. He grabbed my leg and pulled me down again. I kicked him with my free foot. I must have made serious contact, because he howled in pain. I scrambled to my feet and starting running again, but with a limp this time. I'd really banged up my knee on that last fall.

I reached the main street just in time to see a bus lumbering to a stop on the other side of the street. I dashed through traffic to reach it. By then it was pulling away from the curb, and the guy who had been chasing me was stopping cars as he darted across the street to get to me. I hammered on the bus door. The driver finally opened it. I jumped on. The doors swooshed shut, and the bus started to move. The guy who had been chasing me pounded his fists on the door, but the bus had picked up speed. It was too late to stop. I looked out through the glass in the door at his snarling face. He stared back at me and held up his hand, making a gesture as if he were shooting me. I dropped a ticket into the fare box and found a seat near the back of the bus, where I looked out the window again. The guy was still looking at the bus. He was giving it the finger.

I thought about that guy all night after the break-in at the Ashdales. Those Nine-Eight guys are tough. They play for keeps. And they don't let anyone get away with disrespecting them or butting into their business, like I had done. What if they'd caught up with Tilo, if not that day, then some other time? What if they'd pressured him to tell where I was living? Did Tilo even know? I couldn't remember if I had told him or not. What if I had? Would he have told those guys? Or would he have kept his mouth shut? After all, I had done my best to help him out. But maybe he didn't know that. He'd disappeared into an alley before I stuck out my foot. He hadn't seen me trip up those guys.

Thinking about the Nine-Eights was enough to make me check out the street before I left for the youth center the next morning. It was enough to make me look over my shoulder the whole way there. I thought about all the other kids who were involved in programs at the youth center. Had any of them been involved with the Nine-Eights? Did any of them still know Nine-Eight members? If anyone asked them about me, would they tell? Would some Nine-Eights be waiting for me when I got to the youth center? Or would they jump me on my way home? I started to wish I'd never gone to visit Mrs. Girardi.

Nobody followed me to the youth center. No one was waiting for me there either. I breathed a huge sigh of relief when I looked around the place and saw the same old people who had been there all summer. Then DeVon waved me over.

"Hey, Ethan," he said, "someone came by looking for you yesterday."

I gulped. My worst nightmare was coming true. I tried to hide what I was feeling, but it was hard, because I was shaking all over.

Chapter Five

"Who was it?" I asked DeVon.

"A cop."

I almost laughed out loud.

"A cop?" I said.

"Yeah."

Not a Nine-Eight. A cop. Cops I could handle, especially now.

"What did he want?"

"He was asking about you—you know, how long you've been in the program, how long some of the counselors here have known you, whether you were still involved with any gangs, stuff like that."

It sounded like Officer Firelli hadn't given up believing that I was somehow behind what had happened at the Ashdales' house yesterday.

"What did you tell him?" I asked.

"What could I tell him?" DeVon said. "I haven't known you that long, so I had to make up all kinds of bull about you—you know, how you show up every day on time, how you've been taking the program seriously, how you've changed the way you look at some things, how your pictures are among the best in the program." He grinned at me. Everything he'd told Firelli was true—well, except for the last part.

"What do you mean, *among* the best?" I said. "I thought I *was* the best."

"I also told him how modest and unassuming you were," DeVon said. Then he got serious. "Is there anything going on that I should know about, Ethan?"

"What do you mean?"

"Cops don't come around asking about kids unless *something* is happening."

"My house was broken into yesterday," I said. "It was probably about that."

"He didn't ask about anything like that," DeVon said. "He just asked about you, and I told him what I know—the whole truth and nothing but the truth."

"What did he say?"

"Not much. But he was really interested in the Picture This program. He asked me what it was all about. He asked me about the projects kids were working on. He wanted to see some of the pictures they'd taken—especially yours."

I could imagine Firelli being curious about what kind of pictures I had taken.

He probably thought they would be weird and morbid.

"Did you show him?"

"How could I?" DeVon said. "I had to tell him that as long as you've been in the program, you've never backed up a single photo, even though I nag you and nag you. You're going to be sorry, Ethan. All you have to do is drop that camera or lose it, and all the work you've done will be gone forever."

"I don't want anyone looking at my stuff," I said.

"So put a password on it. I'm not kidding, Ethan. You don't want to lose everything, do you?"

"I'll think about it," I said. "First I want to look at what I have and work out how I want to present it."

"Suit yourself," DeVon said.

I was glad that I hadn't backed up my pictures onto the youth center computer. I was proud of the pictures

I had taken, but I didn't want Officer Firelli looking at them, especially without my permission.

"I'll back everything up as soon as I have all the shots I need," I said. "I promise."

DeVon sighed. "Promises, promises," he said. "If I had a nickel for every promise that was ever made to me…" He didn't finish his sentence. He didn't have to. I'd heard it dozens of times before. DeVon would be a millionaire.

Sara came up to me after that. She's so small and innocent-looking that it was hard to imagine how she ended up in the program.

"That cop looked at my pictures," she said. "He asked me about you."

"Yeah?" I liked Sara. If I had more nerve, I would have asked her out. "What did you say?"

"A cop asks questions? What do you think I said?"

I had no idea. That was part of the problem. If I knew how she felt about me, maybe I could decide whether to ask her out.

"I said all good stuff, of course," she said. "How you're serious about the program. How you take your camera everywhere in case you see something you want to shoot. How you're into running." She smiled. "How I see you running in the cemetery ravine every Sunday morning."

"You do?" That was news to me. I had never seen her.

"Yeah," she said. "And how sometimes you stop dead in your tracks, take out your camera and take a picture." She smiled again. "Like I said, all good stuff."

I smiled back at her. Maybe I would ask her out. It looked like she might say yes.

Mrs. Ashdale called my name as soon I let myself into the house late that afternoon. I found her sitting in her reading chair in the living room. Mrs. Ashdale was always reading, and I don't mean lightweight stuff. She always had a couple of books on the go. Usually they were big fat books with hard covers on topics like history or politics or psychology or the environment. She was the smartest woman I had ever met. But she wasn't reading when I went to see what she wanted. She was sitting quietly in her chair with her hands in her lap. Something was wrong.

"Officer Firelli came by this afternoon," she said.

Boy, that cop sure got around.

"What did he want?" I said. "Did he find out anything about who trashed the house?"

Mrs. Ashdale didn't say anything for a few seconds. She just looked at me, like she was wondering about something. But what?

"He said he talked to some people he knew in your old neighborhood," she said at last. "Ethan, is there anything you want to tell me?"

What was she talking about?

"About what?" I said.

She sighed. I knew by then that this wasn't a good sign.

"He told me that he had it on good authority that you were in some kind of fight a few weeks ago. He said it involved a gang. Is that true?"

I knew Officer Firelli always thought the worst of me. He didn't like me. Well, guess what? I didn't like him either.

"Not exactly," I said.

"Sit down, Ethan," Mrs. Ashdale said.

I sat.

"What happened?" she said. "Why didn't you tell Bill or me about it?"

"Because I didn't think it was important," I said. "It was just one of those things."

I told her exactly what had happened. She listened without interrupting. When I had finished, she said, "I can understand why you wanted to help your friend. But it sounds like that boy who chased you was really angry. Do you think he would come looking for you? Do you think he would try to get even for what you did?"

I wanted to tell her no. I wanted to tell her it was no big deal, because I didn't want her to worry—not about me. I liked Mrs. Ashdale. I also didn't want anything to happen that might make the Ashdales decide that they didn't want to be my foster parents anymore. But I couldn't lie to her, not now, not after what Officer Firelli had told her.

"I don't know," I said. It was the truth. "Those guys have a reputation, you know?"

She nodded.

"But I went over it and over it, and I'm pretty sure I didn't tell anyone I used to hang around with that I'm living here now. And I did what everyone told me to do—I put all that stuff behind me. I only went back there to see Mrs. Girardi."

"I'm going to have to tell Bill about this," she said.

That made me feel sick inside. Was she mad at me? Was she going to try to get rid of me?

"We want you to be safe, Ethan. You've been doing well since you've been living here, and Mrs. Girardi told us that she thinks you're a good boy."

"You talked to Mrs. Girardi about me?" She had never mentioned that.

"Of course, we did." She didn't sound mad at all. "She was sad that she had to let you go. She wanted us to promise that we'd take good care of you. But that's not easy to do if you don't tell us everything. You understand that, don't you?"

I nodded. I was ashamed that I hadn't told her right away about the Nine-Eights.

"If you see any of those boys, you're to tell Bill or me right away. Okay?"

"Okay," I said.

"Promise?"

"I promise."

"And there's nothing else you want to tell me?"

I shook my head. Now she knew it all.

I hoped that I would never see a Nine-Eight again. But hoping for something doesn't make it true.

Chapter Six

"Don't forget tomorrow," Mrs. Ashdale said after supper that night.

"Tomorrow?" I said.

"Check the fridge."

I went to the big calendar on the fridge, and there it was. *Ethan, Dr. Finstead, 11:00 AM. Ethan and Anna, Eaton Centre, lunch*. I groaned. Dr. Finstead was a dentist. When I lived with my dad, I never went to the dentist. The first thing Mrs. Girardi had done when I went to live with her was make an appointment. It turned out I had a lot of cavities. It took three visits to get them all filled. That's when I decided that I didn't like going to the dentist. I hated the sound the drill made. I also hated the smell that filled the air when the dentist was drilling my teeth. It made me sick to my stomach. But Mrs. Ashdale was even more fanatical about dentists than Mrs. Girardi had been. Her rule was that all of us had to go twice a year for a checkup and cleaning. She was also very big on flossing.

So I went to the dentist. The dental hygienist scraped the plaque from my teeth. Next, she cleaned them with a little machine that made a high-pitched sound. Then she polished them. By the time she had finished, I was rinsing blood out of my mouth. But my teeth felt terrific.

I couldn't stop running my tongue over them.

Then the dentist checked me out. I held my breath as she poked and prodded to see if I had any cavities.

"You're all good, Ethan," she said finally. She sent me on my way with a new toothbrush, a little container of dental floss and a follow-up appointment in another six months.

From there I headed to the Eaton Centre to meet Mrs. Ashdale. Alan's birthday was coming up, and she wanted me to help her pick out a present for him. We were going out for lunch after. Believe it or not, I was looking forward to it. I liked spending time with Mrs. Ashdale. Not only was she nice, but she was also interesting to talk to. I always learned something new. Most of the time she said things that made me think.

I was supposed to meet her outside the mall entrance. I glanced at my watch.

I was ten minutes early. But I headed down there to wait anyway. There was always something going on outside the mall—guys doing sketches of passers-by for ten or twenty bucks, musicians, some of them actually pretty good, busking for coins, chalk artists putting together huge sidewalk "paintings," that kind of thing.

I strolled down the sidewalk, looking at the charcoal portraits of Jimi Hendrix, John Lennon, John Wayne and Brad Pitt that one of the artists had laid out to show people how good he was. Then, I'm not even sure why, it was just one of those things, I glanced across the street. There was a big square there with a stage at one end. Sometimes there were free concerts sponsored by a local radio station. But most of the time people just hung out over there, eating street dogs or take-out food from the mall if it was a nice day. Maybe that's why I glanced over there—to see if there was anything special going on. My heart slammed to a stop at what I saw.

It was the guy who had chased me onto the bus back in Mrs. Girardi's neighborhood.

He wasn't alone.

The two guys I had tripped were with him. So were four or five other guys, all of them from the Nine-Eights. They were standing in front of the square, not caring that they were blocking the whole sidewalk. They didn't notice the dirty looks people gave them when they had to step out onto the street to get past. They were too busy scanning the crowd on my side of the street, like they were looking for someone. I ducked my head immediately. I had to get out of there.

Still with my head down, I turned and glanced up the street. Mrs. Ashdale was standing at the corner on the other side, waiting for the light to change. Everything happened fast after that.

I was thinking that I should make a run for the corner so that I could head off Mrs. Ashdale. Then I heard someone shout, and I couldn't help myself. I turned toward the sound. Some of the people on my side of the street were standing like statues and staring at the other side of the street. Other people were scurrying away. I looked across the street and saw why. Standing right in among the Nine-Eights was a scruffy-looking guy with a hat pulled down low over his head. He had a gun in his hand. It was pointed across the street. And it went off.

Blam!

People screamed. People ran. Traffic ground to a halt. I heard a loud bang. This one was different—it sounded like two cars colliding.

Blam!

Something whizzed by me.

"Ethan!" someone yelled. Mrs. Ashdale.

I threw myself to the sidewalk.

The Nine-Eights were still in front of
the square, but now they were looking
around, like they couldn't figure out what
had happened. The scruffy man with the
hat had disappeared.

Sirens sounded.

The Nine-Eights looked at each other.
Then they ran.

A cop car showed up. Then another
and another.

I got to my feet. Mrs. Ashdale rushed
toward me and grabbed me by the
shoulders. She looked me over, then
threw her arms around me and hugged
me. It wasn't until later that night that
I realized why she had done that. She'd
been scared that I was hurt, and when she
saw that I was okay, she was relieved.
She really cared about me.

"Someone could have been killed,"
she said. She kept saying it, like she
couldn't believe what had happened.
I couldn't believe it either.

"Those Nine-Eights don't care about anyone who isn't one of them," I said.

"What?" Mrs. Ashdale looked at me, surprised. "You know who did the shooting?"

"I didn't recognize the guy with the gun," I said. "But those guys he was with, those were Nine-Eights."

More sirens sounded. People were swirling around us. Cops were getting out of cars. They spread out, trying to get everyone calmed down and, I guess, trying to find people who had seen what had happened and might be able to tell them about it.

"Officer," Mrs. Ashdale called. "Officer!"

A cop turned toward her.

"My son saw what happened," Mrs. Ashdale said.

Son? I had never heard her call me that before. It sounded good when she said it.

I wasn't the only one who heard her.

"Well, well," a familiar voice said. "Look who's here."

It was Officer Firelli.

"The kid saw what happened," the first cop said.

"Did he?" Officer Firelli nodded to Mrs. Ashdale. "Ma'am," he said, one of those people who was polite to adults but not to kids. "You saw who did the shooting, Ethan?"

I nodded.

"Do you know their names?"

"No."

"But you've seen them before?"

"Yes."

Officer Firelli looked around. "Show me exactly where you were standing."

I went back to where I had been when the shooting started.

"Okay, Ethan," he said. "A detective is going to want to speak to you."

He told the first cop to keep an eye on me. He said he'd be right back.

An hour later, I was at the police station with Mrs. Ashdale, giving a statement to a detective named Catton. Officer Firelli was listening. After I had finished talking, Catton said, "So you recognized at least three of the guys on the other side of the street, is that right?"

"Yes."

"And as far as you know, those three and the others they were with are all members of the gang called the Nine-Eights?"

I nodded.

"But you don't know their names?"

"No."

"Officer Firelli tells me you had a run-in with some of those guys a few weeks ago. Do you think they were shooting at you?"

"I don't know," I said. I sure hoped not.

"Did you see any of the gang members with a gun?"

"No."

"But you did see another man with a gun, a man with the hat whose face you didn't see, but that you're pretty sure isn't a gang member, is that right?"

"Yeah. He wasn't dressed right. And he seemed older."

"I thought you didn't see his face."

"The way he dressed—it looked like an old guy," I said. "Maybe around your age."

Detective Catton leaned back in his chair and sighed. He glanced at Officer Firelli before turning back to me.

"I understand you've had some gang involvement, Ethan," he said.

"That's in the past," Mrs. Ashdale said firmly.

"Please, ma'am," Catton said, as polite to her as Officer Firelli had been.

"Ethan needs to answer these questions himself." He looked at me.

"I used to hang around with some guys," I admitted.

"Who were rivals of the Nine-Eights," Catton said.

"Yeah. But I was never a gang member. I got out of that."

Another cop waved at Officer Firelli, who got up and went over to him. He was back a few minutes later, whispering in Catton's ear. Catton was silent for a minute. Then he fixed me with a somber look.

"Are you sure you've told me everything, Ethan?" he said.

What was going on?

"Yes," I said.

"And you answered all of my questions truthfully?"

"Yes." I really had.

"I know how it is with gangs, Ethan. I know that people don't like to speak out about what they've seen when there are gangs involved. They're afraid what might happen to them."

"I'm not afraid," I said.

"But you told me you didn't see any of the Nine-Eights with a gun," he said. "Just some man with a hat that you've never seen before. Is that right?"

"Yes." What did he want from me? Did he want me to make up stuff?

"We have other witnesses who saw one of the gang members with a gun, Ethan."

"That's not what I saw."

"We also have a preliminary report from the firearms examiner. And another from the crime-scene boys. There were two guns, Ethan. We recovered the bullets. We found them a few feet from where you were standing. It looks like you were the target."

Chapter Seven

Mrs. Ashdale gasped.

"You mean, someone was trying to kill Ethan?"

"I'm just saying where we found the bullets, ma'am. And given Ethan's past and recent events…" He turned to me again. "Will you help us, Ethan? Will you look at some pictures and see if you can identify the Nine-Eights who were down on the street today?"

"Of course he will," Mrs. Ashdale said.

Detective Catton was right about one thing. Most people are scared to rat out gang members. I'm not that different from most people. I was afraid too.

"There were a lot of people on the street," Mrs. Ashdale told me. "I'm sure the police have spoken to as many of them as they could. And you heard what they said—someone else saw one of the gang members with a gun. I'm sure they've asked that person to look at pictures too. They've probably asked a lot of people. So if the police arrest someone, it's not going to be just because of what you saw, Ethan."

I knew what she said made sense. But it didn't make me feel any better. The Nine-Eights didn't know everyone on the street today. But they knew me.

And some of them already had a grudge against me. But I went with Officer Firelli and I picked out the ones I recognized.

"You did the right thing," Officer Firelli said. "It's a miracle someone wasn't killed or seriously injured. It's a miracle *you* weren't killed. You know that, right, Ethan?"

"Yeah." I glanced at him. "Do you really think they were trying to kill me?"

"You tell me," he said. "Look, I know you've been working hard at changing…"

"Is that what they told you at the youth center?" I asked.

He frowned. "What youth center?"

"The one where I go to my program." Officer Firelli gave me a blank look. Nice try. "I know you were there. I know you were asking about me."

"Not me," Officer Firelli said. "The only person I spoke to was your foster mother, and she had nothing but good things to say about you." He dug in his pocket and pulled out a business card. "If you see any of those gang members around or if you get scared and just want to talk, call me. I mean it, Ethan."

Right. Like I was going to call a cop who didn't even like me. That would be the day.

Before we left, Mrs. Ashdale quizzed Officer Firelli and Detective Catton about my safety.

"What if some of those gang members come around?" she said. "What if they still want to hurt Ethan?"

"After what happened today, they'll be lying low for a while," Detective Catton said. "But we'll have someone keep an eye on your house tonight. If you see anything, anything at all, call us."

It was late by the time we left the police station. Mrs. Ashdale wanted to go back to the mall to buy Alan's birthday present. I asked her if she would mind if I didn't go with her.

"I don't blame you for not wanting to go back there," she said. "But I'd feel better if you were with me."

"I want to stop by the youth center," I said. "Then I'll go straight home, I promise." Mr. Ashdale was at home with Alan and Tricia. "I'll call you on your cell when I get there if you want."

"That would be much appreciated," she said.

She headed back to the mall. I headed for the youth center. DeVon was there. He was always there.

"What's up, Ethan?" he said. "Come to work on your project?"

I shook my head.

"It's about that cop who was here the other day asking about me," I said. "Did he tell you his name?"

"He did," DeVon said. "But I don't

remember. I saw his badge though. Why?"

"Was it Firelli?"

DeVon thought for a moment. "No," he said, "it wasn't an Italian name. It was something ordinary, like Mason or Manson, something like that. I'm pretty sure it started with an *M*. Or maybe an *N*."

"But it wasn't Firelli?"

"Definitely not Firelli." He peered at me. "Is everything okay, Ethan?"

"Yeah. Everything's fine." At least, it was if you didn't count the fact that someone was trying to kill me.

It should have come as no surprise that I had trouble getting to sleep that night. I kept thinking about what Detective Catton had said. There had been two shooters and two guns, both aimed at me. It was a miracle I hadn't been killed. It was a miracle no one else had been killed either. I started to shake all over.

I kept thinking about what had happened.

Then I thought: how had the Nine-Eights found me? Was it just a coincidence that they happened to be walking down the other side of the street at exactly the time I was standing there? Was it some weird kind of accident that they looked over and saw me standing there?

Except that wasn't the way it had happened. When I first noticed them, they had been standing near the square, scanning the crowd on my side of the street. They had been looking for *someone*. Had they been looking for me? But how could they have known I was going to be at the Eaton Centre? I started to shake even harder. Had they been watching the Ashdales' house? Had they followed me and Mrs. Ashdale downtown? Had they been planning all along to shoot me?

What if they were watching the house now? What if they were waiting for me the next morning when I left the home?

And what about the other man I had seen, the one who looked like he didn't belong? I had definitely seen a gun in *his* hand. Who was he? And why had *he* shot at me?

What was going on?

I stayed inside the whole of the next day. I don't know how many times I peeked out the windows. Maybe dozens. Maybe hundreds.

The phone rang just before dinner. Mr. Ashdale answered it. He was on the phone for a long time. When he finally hung up, he came into the kitchen, where I was helping Mrs. Ashdale make a salad.

"That was an Officer Firelli," he said. "He called to let us know that they had made some arrests based on the identifications made by you and some other witnesses."

Mrs. Ashdale breathed a sigh of relief.

"Thank goodness that's over," she said.

Mr. Ashdale and I looked at each other. I could tell by the grim look on his face that he was thinking the same thing I was—it wasn't anywhere near over. The cops had made some arrests. They had picked up some guys on weapons charges. But no one had been killed. No one had even been hurt. It was just a matter of time before the guys who had been arrested were let out on bail—and probably not very much time either. Then what? If they really had been shooting at me, what if they decided to try again? And what if, next time, they didn't miss?

Chapter Eight

Mrs. Ashdale talked to Officer Firelli the next day. Most of the guys the cops had arrested were already out on bail, with strict conditions. The only one who had been detained was the Nine-Eight who had chased me to the bus. Apparently this wasn't his first weapons charge.

I felt like one of those teenagers in a horror movie. I kept holding my breath and looking over my shoulder. Mrs. Ashdale drove me to the community center for the next couple of days and picked me up in the afternoon on her way to get Alan and Tricia from camp. While I was there, I stayed inside. I didn't even leave the building to pick up a pizza slice or some fries for lunch with the others from the Picture This program. I also stayed in all night every night.

Nothing happened.

By the end of the week, I had relaxed a little. Maybe Detective Catton was right. Maybe the Nine-Eights were scared to come after me again so soon. Maybe they knew the cops would go straight to them if anything happened to me. Maybe they thought I wasn't worth it. After all, I didn't live in the area anymore and never set foot in their territory.

By the next Sunday, just over a week after the shooting, my life went back to normal. I got up that morning, put on my sneakers and slipped my camera into a fanny pack.

"Going to the ravine?" Mrs. Ashdale asked me.

I nodded. I went for a run in the ravine every Sunday morning. Right afterward, I spent time in the cemetery. It was the biggest and oldest one in the city. Lots of famous people were buried there. I'd discovered it when I moved in with the Ashdales. I'd also found out that it was a great place to take pictures—of gravestones and mausoleums, of trees and flowers and birds, and of people. Especially of people. All kinds of people came and stood in front of the graves of people they knew. You'd think that most of them would be sad, but not all of them were, not by a long shot. That was what fascinated me. I had started taking a series of pictures of those people. So far I had people who looked sad, people who were crying and people who looked lost. I also had people who looked smug, people who were nodding with satisfaction, and one man who was smiling at the name on the headstone he was looking at.

"Maybe you should ask Bill to go with you," Mrs. Ashdale said.

"I'll be fine." Besides, Sunday was Mr. Ashdale's day to catch up on his newspapers. He loved to read the papers but didn't always have time. On Sunday he drank coffee and read his way through the pile that had accumulated during the week.

"At least take my cell phone," Mrs. Ashdale said. "Just in case."

I didn't want her to worry, so I tucked it into the pocket of my shorts. Then I set out for the ravine.

As usual, there were a few other runners down there and a few people walking their dogs. And, as usual, I was surprised that the place wasn't crammed with people. It was so peaceful down there. It was the next best thing to being out in the country.

I ran the same route I always did. I started across the street from the south end of the cemetery and ran down the path alongside the river. The first half of the run was always the easiest. It was a gentle downhill slope all the way. Then came the loop, a long curve away from the road and away from the river. I hardly ever saw anyone down there, and that Sunday was no exception. There were days when I wished that loop would go on forever and that I would never see another person. I breathed in deeply. All I could hear was the crunch of my sneakers on the gravel path and the song of birds from the treetops on either side of me. I couldn't help thinking about Sara. She'd said she had seen me running down here before. I wondered if she would see me today—and if I would see her.

I knew I was halfway through my run when I saw the gate up ahead. It was always padlocked, and it blocked access to the massive houses that perched on top of the ravine. You couldn't see the houses this time of year, when the trees were covered in leaves. But in winter, through the naked branches, they were impossible to miss. They were all massive, and they sat on a ravine-side road in the most expensive part of the city. I'd never seen any of those houses from the front, but when I ran in winter, I always imagined what it must be like for the people living up there. I imagined them cozy and warm, sipping cocoa and looking out over the treetops. It must be like living in the country.

I was approaching the gate when it happened. My foot got tangled up on something, and I went crashing to the ground. I threw out my hands to break my fall. They hit the gravel and skidded. I felt sharp pebbles biting into the palms of my hands. Then my knees hit, hard, and a searing pain shot up both my legs. I was on my hands and knees, wondering what I had tripped on, when everything went black. Someone had put some kind of hood over my head so that I couldn't see. Then I felt something slip over the hood and tighten around my neck. I panicked.

I grabbed at whatever was around my neck. It was a rope. I tried to loosen it, but instead it got tighter.

A voice said, "If you struggle or make a noise, you'll be sorry."

Then someone jerked hard on the rope, almost choking me.

"Get up," he said.

I tried again to get my hands on the rope. The man jerked on it again, tightening it even more.

"Get up," he said.

I got up. He grabbed one of my arms and started tugging at me. I tripped. His fingers bit into my arm as he hauled me to my feet. He shoved me ahead of him, holding me so that I didn't fall again. Something brushed against my leg. That's when I realized that I wasn't on the gravel path anymore.

The man slammed me against something. A car. He jerked my arms behind my back and tied them with the same rope that he had slipped around my neck. I tried to struggle, but when I did, the rope tightened around my neck. I heard a throaty chuckle. What was going on? Who was this man? What was he going to do with me?

He grabbed me by my tied hands and yanked me away from the car. I listened hard, trying to figure out what was going on. I heard a sound, like the trunk of a car popping open. Then the man shoved me forward again so that my head and shoulders were inside the trunk. He grabbed my legs. I kicked hard to try to stop him. The rope around my neck got tighter. The man was strong. He shoved my legs into the trunk. Then he slammed the trunk shut, and I felt myself go cold all over. I was going to die.

Chapter Nine

I tried to fight back the terror that surged through me. Where was he taking me? Why had he grabbed me in the first place? I squirmed and struggled, and then panicked again when the rope around my neck got tighter. I forced myself to lie still. I pushed my arms up my back as far as I could to release some of the pressure on the rope. It worked. But

I still felt panicky. The hood over my head made it hard to breathe, and the air in the trunk was hot and stale. I began to worry that the trunk was airtight and I would use up all the air before I got wherever we were going.

I remembered that I had Mrs. Ashdale's cell phone in the pocket of my shorts. I tried to reach it with my hand. But that just tightened the rope again, and I had to reposition my hands and arms so that I could breathe.

At first the car stopped and started a lot. That had to mean we were still in the city; he was stopping for red lights and stop signs. I twisted myself onto my back. Every time the car stopped, I kicked the lid of the trunk as hard as I could with both feet, over and over again. I yelled for help. I prayed that someone would hear me and call the police.

Then there were no more stops, and I knew we were on the highway.

I tried to stay calm. Maybe someone had heard. Maybe someone had called the cops and given them the license number of the car. Maybe someone would come to my rescue.

The car kept moving. It seemed to be going faster and faster.

Panic crept over me again.

After what seemed like an eternity, the car slowed down a little.

Then it turned onto a bumpy road, and I heard pebbles *ping* against the hubcaps.

The bumpy road turned washboardy, and I was jarred and jostled inside the trunk.

Finally the car stopped. I held my breath. Now what?

I heard a car door open and then close again. The trunk popped open and cool fresh air flooded in. Rough hands grabbed me, yanking me out of the trunk and dumping me onto the ground. The hood was ripped off my head.

I felt like I was going to throw up. Blood rushed to my head, and my knees wobbled. I stared at the man who had hauled me out of the trunk. I was sure I recognized his cold, hard eyes and small, mean mouth. I was sure he was the same man who had held me up in the alley. But why? And why had he brought me here?

He pushed me over to a birch tree and forced me down into a sitting position. My tailbone landed on something sharp. I let out a yelp. The man ignored it and tied me to the trunk of the tree. When he had finished, he unbuckled my fanny pack and opened it. He pulled out my camera and turned it on. He scrolled quickly through the pictures. He must have come to one that interested him, because he stopped and stared at it.

Then he dropped the camera onto a rock and started to stomp on it with one booted foot. He stomped and stomped until my camera was smashed to pieces. Then he went back to the car and got a shovel out of the backseat. He started to dig a hole. This couldn't be happening to me. It just couldn't.

"Why?" I said. The word came out of me the way it might come out of a frog, like a croak.

The man didn't even look at me. He just kept digging.

"Is it because I wouldn't give you my backpack?" I said.

He paused in his digging and looked at me.

"You should have handed it over like you were told, Ethan," he said. I stared at him. He knew my name. "If you had, we wouldn't be here right now."

"But there was nothing in it," I said.

He started digging again.

I looked at my smashed-up camera. Is that what he had been after the whole time? I glanced at him again.

"It was you who went by the youth center asking about me, wasn't it?" I said.

He didn't answer. But it must have been him. He'd asked DeVon about the program. He'd asked to see my pictures.

DeVon had told him I never backed my pictures up.

Sara had told him I always had my camera with me when I ran in the ravine on Sunday morning.

"You shot at me outside the Eaton Centre too," I said. It had to have been him. "How did you know I would be there?"

He shook his head. "I do my homework, Ethan," he said. "I always do my homework."

"But the Nine-Eights," I said. "How did they know?"

Then I remembered Mrs. Ashdale's fridge calendar. It had been on the floor after the break-in. Whoever had trashed the house must have seen it. My dentist appointment had been on it. So had the Eaton Centre.

The man's mouth turned up into a smile. "Someone must have told them," he said.

Someone? He meant himself. *He* had put the Nine-Eights on me.

I sat there, my brain reeling, watching the man dig. He was going to kill me. I was sure of it. But why? What had I ever done to him? And what did my camera have to do with anything?

While he dug, I tried to untie the rope around my wrists. It was tight. And my butt was sore from whatever I had landed on when he pushed me down. I shifted positions as much as I could and felt behind me. No wonder my butt was sore. I'd been sitting on a sharp piece of rock.

A really sharp piece.

I maneuvered my wrists so that they were against the rock's sharpest edge. I started to move them up and down, up and down, carefully so that the man wouldn't see what I was doing, but firmly so that maybe, with some luck, the rock would bite into the rope.

Up and down.

Up and down.

Sweat started to pour off me.

I'd never been so scared in my life.

The man dug and dug. He hummed while he worked. He was enjoying himself. He wasn't the least bit worried that he would be interrupted. He had chosen this spot well.

Up and down.

Up and down.

The hole got deeper and deeper. It got longer too. Just the right size for a person.

For me.

Up and down.

Up and...

I could feel the rope starting to give, but not nearly enough. The man climbed up out of the hole.

"Please," I said. "Let me go. I won't say anything. I swear. Please just let me go."

The man's cold, hard eyes peered at me.

"Really, Ethan," he said. "How stupid do you think I am?"

He planted the shovel into the pile of dirt he had dug out of it and went over to the car. I continued to rub the rope against the rock while he opened the car door and leaned across the front seat. My eyes were burning. I felt like I was going to cry. I felt even worse when the man backed out of the car. He was holding a gun in his hand. I froze up. He tucked the gun into the back of his pants and started toward me.

Chapter Ten

I kept my hands perfectly still behind my back when the man circled around me and undid the rope that was tied around the birch tree. He grabbed me by one arm and yanked me to my feet.

"Get moving," he said, shoving me toward the hole.

I stumbled and fell.

"Get up," the man said, his voice as hard and cold as his eyes. He grabbed my elbow and pulled me roughly to my feet. As he did, I felt the rope holding my hands give way. I was so surprised that I didn't know what to do.

"I said move," he said, pushing me again.

I did what he said, and I stumbled again, this time on purpose. I yanked my hands as far apart as I could. The rope fell to the ground. I grabbed the shovel with both hands and spun around. The man had one hand behind his back. He was reaching for his gun. I swung the shovel like a baseball bat and hit him square on the side of his head. He fell to the ground with a groan. He was out cold.

I took the gun gingerly from his hand. I groped in his pockets for his car keys. I checked him again. He was breathing, but he wasn't moving.

I put the gun in the trunk of the car and slammed it shut. I threw the car keys as far as I could into the woods. Then I tied the man's hands behind his back and tied his ankles together. I stared down at his face. There was something familiar about it, but I couldn't tell if that was because I had seen him before or because he just looked like someone I had seen around. Why would someone I didn't know have been trying to kill me?

I dug Mrs. Ashdale's cell phone out of my pocket. Something else came out with it—the card that Officer Firelli had given me. I dialed the number on it, and after a few moments I was put through to Officer Firelli.

"Someone just tried to kill me again," I said. Even I heard the tremble in my voice. "I think it was the same man I saw downtown. He was going to shoot me. He was—"

"Slow down, Ethan," Officer Firelli said. "Are you okay?"

"I guess so," I said.

"What about this man? Is he in a position to hurt you?"

"I hit him with a shovel. He's unconscious. I tied him up."

"Where are you, Ethan?"

"I don't know. Somewhere out in the country."

"Where out in the country? Look around, Ethan. See if you recognize anything or see any landmarks."

I looked all around me. I couldn't believe it. I'd been too scared to realize it at first, but I knew exactly where I was. I was near the tree where the hawks nested, the same hawks whose pictures I had been taking for the past couple of weeks. I told Officer Firelli how to find me.

"Sit tight, Ethan," he said. "I'm going to get someone there as fast as I can.

And I'll get up there as soon as I can too. How's your cell-phone battery?"

I checked it. "It's good."

"Okay. Just stay where you are. If anything happens, call me. Okay, Ethan?"

"Okay."

Two other cop cars arrived first. Officer Firelli must have talked to them, because they knew my name. One of the cops looked me over and asked me if I was okay. Two more cops checked on the man I had tied up. When they shook him, he groaned and opened his eyes, but just for a minute.

"We'd better get him to a hospital," one of the cops said. He went to radio for an ambulance.

Another cop dug into the man's pants pocket and pulled out a wallet. He shook his head as he went through it.

"The guy's a cop," he said. "From the city. His name is Miller. Robert Miller."

"That name sounds familiar," one of the cops said. But he couldn't seem to remember why.

The other three cops looked at me, like all of a sudden they weren't sure who the bad guy was.

"Tell us exactly what happened," one of them said.

They were still looking suspiciously at me when I finished my story, as if they thought I was the one who had been digging the grave for the man and not the other way around. But what kind of sense did that make? I'd called the police. I wouldn't have done that it I was going to kill anyone.

Officer Firelli showed up right behind the ambulance. He introduced himself to the other cops and watched as the man was loaded into the ambulance. One of the cop cars followed it to the hospital. The other two cops stayed to talk to Officer Firelli.

"The kid knocked out a cop," one of them said.

Officer Firelli looked surprised.

"His name is Miller," said the cop who had found Miller's ID.

"Robert Miller?" Officer Firelli said. He looked even more surprised.

"You know him?" the cop said.

Officer Firelli nodded. "We're in the same division. He made the news about a week ago. His wife is missing. Her sister called the police. Miller said he and his wife had a big fight and split up, but the sister isn't buying it. She thinks something's wrong."

"He kidnapped me from the city," I told Officer Firelli. "He brought me out here and tied me up while he dug that hole. Then he took out a gun. He was going to shoot me."

"What did you do with the gun, Ethan?"

"I locked it in the trunk."

He held out his hand. "Give me the keys."

"I threw them away."

Officer Firelli stared at me. I was afraid he didn't believe me. Then he said, "Tell me everything that happened."

So I did. I told him about being kidnapped. I showed him the smashed camera. I told him about Miller mugging me in the alley. "He had a gun then too," I said. "But I didn't think it was real until he shot at me."

"He shot at you?" Officer Firelli said. "Did you tell the Ashdales about this?"

I shook my head. "I thought he was some crazy meth-head or something. I didn't want to worry them."

"You told me on the phone that you think he's the guy who shot at you downtown."

I nodded.

"Well, if that's true," Officer Firelli said, "and if he had the same gun today as he did last week, ballistics should have no trouble matching it."

"He knew where to find me," I said. I told him how I thought that had happened. "He was waiting for me in the ravine."

"But why?" Officer Firelli said. "Why is he so interested in you?"

"I don't know," I said. "In the alley, he was ready to shoot me over my backpack. I tried to tell him there was nothing in it."

"Nothing?"

"Just my camera."

"Your camera?"

I explained what I had been doing all summer.

"But I don't know why he'd be so interested in that," I told Officer Firelli.

"*Was* he interested?"

"A cop went to the youth center and asked the program director if he could see the pictures I'd taken."

"Did the program director show him your pictures?"

"He couldn't. They were in my camera. I hadn't backed them up. DeVon—that's the program director—is always bugging me about that, but I don't like people to see my stuff until I'm ready to show it."

"I'd like to take a look at that camera," Officer Firelli said.

"You can't. He smashed it." I showed him what was left of it.

Officer Firelli sighed. "I guess we're just going to have to wait until Miller wakes up," he said.

I looked at Officer Firelli. I thought about what he had told the other cops about Miller. I thought about the shovel I'd hit Miller with. An idea took shape in my head.

"You don't have to wait," I said.

Chapter Eleven

Because it was Sunday, Officer Firelli had to track down the director of the youth center at home. He asked him to come to the youth center and let us in. He also asked the director to find DeVon and get him to join us.

The director unlocked the youth center door. Then he unlocked the door to the Picture This room. I turned on the computer. The director had to type in a password before we could get to any files.

"DeVon said if anything happened to my camera, I'd lose all my pictures," I said. "So for once I listened to him. I backed everything up on Friday before I went home."

I clicked with the mouse. Another password box came up, and this time I typed in the password. Officer Firelli pulled up a chair and sat down next to me.

"Show me everything that was in your camera," he said.

I showed him my pictures one by one. He was a lot smarter than I thought. He recognized where they had been taken.

"That's where we found you today," he said.

I nodded.

Officer Firelli frowned.

"Why would Miller be interested in pictures of trees and hawks?" he said.

"I don't think he was," I said. I kept clicking through my pictures until I found the one I was looking for.

Suddenly Officer Firelli perked up when he saw it. He pointed to a small figure in one corner of the frame. It was a man holding a shovel—the same man that Mrs. Ashdale had noticed and asked me about. Officer Firelli squinted at him.

"Can you make that bigger?" he said.

I increased the size of the picture and stared at the man with the shovel. My hunch had been right. It was the same person who had been digging my grave a few hours ago. It was Robert Miller.

DeVon arrived. Officer Firelli asked him to describe the police officer who had come to the youth center to ask about me. The person DeVon described sounded an awful lot like Robert Miller. Then Officer Firelli asked him to look at the picture on the computer screen.

"That's him," DeVon said. "That's the cop who was here."

Officer Firelli stared at the picture again. He said, "You see where that picture was taken? Do you think you could find that spot, Ethan?"

"Sure." I'd spent so much time out in those woods that I knew the area like I knew my own room. I didn't ask him why. I already had a pretty good idea.

Officer Firelli made a few calls. Then he phoned Mrs. Ashdale and told her that I was with him and that I was helping him with a police investigation. He said she shouldn't worry, that I hadn't done anything wrong. He told her that he would have me back home in a few hours. Before we left the youth center, we printed out a couple of copies of the two photos that had Robert Miller in them.

We drove back out to the woods where I had photographed the hawks. I looked at the photos. Using the hawks' nesting tree as a landmark, I led Officer Firelli to the place where Robert Miller had been standing when I had accidentally taken his picture. Officer Firelli told me to stand off to one side while he examined the ground.

Some police cars showed up. So did a police forensics van. Officer Firelli talked to them for a few minutes and let them take over. It wasn't long before one of the cops said, "It looks like we have something here."

Before they touched anything, they took a lot of pictures. Then they started digging. They took even more pictures. Then one of them said, "We've got a body."

Officer Firelli went to talk to the other cops. Then he said, "Come on, Ethan. We'd better get you back home."

"But—"

"It's going to take a while to identify the body, and it's getting late."

He drove me back to the Ashdales. When we got there, he came with me into the house to tell the Ashdales what had happened. Mrs. Ashdale's face went white as she listened. Mr. Ashdale put his arm around her. Officer Firelli promised to tell us what they found out there in the woods.

"Ethan should be safe now," he said. "From what Ethan's told me, Miller realized that his picture had been taken. He was afraid that someone might connect him to that spot in the woods. That's why he tried so hard to get Ethan's camera. When that didn't work, he tried to get rid of Ethan."

For the second time since I came to live with her, Mrs. Ashdale hugged me. It almost made me cry.

Chapter Twelve

It was in the newspaper the next morning, but by then I already knew the whole story. Officer Firelli had called. The body they found in the woods was Eileen Miller, Robert Miller's missing wife. My pictures showed that Miller knew where she was all along. She had been shot with the same gun that Miller had used to shoot at me downtown. The police also found the bullet that he had shot at me in the alley. It was embedded in a door frame.

"It all ties back to Miller. He's going to stand trial for murder, a couple of counts of attempted murder, and kidnapping—unless he gets smart and pleads guilty," Officer Firelli said. "He must have had a good look at you that day in the woods, Ethan. He used to work in your old neighborhood. He picked you up a few times when you were underage—once for shoplifting and once for attempted purse-snatch. You remember?"

I nodded. That explained why I'd had the feeling that I'd seen him before.

"I didn't recognize him," I said.

"Well, he recognized you. We found a copy of your police record at his house. He knew where you were living. He must have followed you when he mugged you in that alley. Then he broke into the house to look for the camera and to check to see if you had backed up your photos on the Ashdales' computer."

"I didn't."

"He figured that out. He also knew about your involvement with the Nine-Eights. One of the guys we arrested said that someone tipped them off that you were downtown. They went there looking for you. Miller took advantage of that. He shot at you."

Shot and missed.

"He also knew about the program you're in at the youth center. It was in your file. And he knew you ran in the ravine every Sunday. A girl at the youth center told him." He meant Sara.

"He must have decided to grab you when he found out that you always had your camera with you but that you never backed up your pictures. He decided he wasn't going to take any chances. He was going to get rid of you and the camera. He must have thought that would put him in the clear. And he was right. We never would have found his wife if you hadn't taken those pictures. He would have gotten away with it. I know how scared you must have been, Ethan, but your photos helped us catch a killer."

A week later, the Picture This program ended with a special showing of our projects. Mine took first prize. The Ashdales were there with Alan and Tricia. So was Officer Firelli. He congratulated me on my work. Sara was there too. She took second prize. She didn't seem to mind that I had beaten her. She held my hand the whole time. I'd decided that you never know what's going to happen, so you shouldn't waste time. I'd asked her out right after Miller was arrested. She'd said yes right away. For once, things were going right for me.

Norah McClintock is the best-selling author of a number of titles in the Orca Soundings series, including *Tell*, *Snitch*, *Down* and *Back*.

The following is an excerpt from
another exciting Orca Soundings novel,
Hannah's Touch by Laura Langston.

Chapter One

A bee sting changed my life. One minute I was normal. The next minute I wasn't.

If you listen to my parents, they'll tell you I haven't been normal since my boyfriend, Logan, died. But they don't get it. When he died, a part of me went with him. Plus, I could have stopped it. The accident that killed him, I mean.

But I was normal. Until it happened.

It was the third Sunday in September, sunny and warm. School was back in. The maple leaves on Seattle's trees were curling like old, arthritic fingers. Fall was only a footstep away.

I wasn't thinking about fall that Sunday. Or school or maple leaves. For sure I wasn't thinking about bees.

I was at work, thinking about Logan, and I was cold. It was freezing in the drugstore. Bentley had the air conditioning cranked to high.

"I swear, Bentley, it's warmer outside than it is in here." We'd run out of Vitamin C, so I was restocking the middle shelf beside the pharmacy. "I don't know why you need the air conditioning on."

"It keeps the air moving." He was behind the counter, slapping the lid on a bottle of yellow pills. "Besides, fall doesn't officially start until September 23." He slid the bottle into a small white bag.

Like that made any difference. But Bentley, who was the pharmacist, was also the boss of Bartell Drugs. As far as he was concerned, summer was sunscreen displays and air conditioning. No matter how cold it got.

I only had to whine a few more seconds. "Take twenty," Bentley said. "It's quiet today."

I grabbed a soda from the cooler by the magazines, waved at Lila, our cashier, and wandered outside. The heat was better than any drug Bentley sold. I popped the tab on my can, took a sip, breathed in sunshine.

"Well, well, just the gal I want to see."

It was Maude O'Connell, leaning on her turquoise walker, her uni-boob and gold chains practically resting on the top bar. An unfortunate orange and blue caftan covered her plus-size body.

"My gout pills ready yet, Hannah?" she asked.

"Behind the counter and waiting, M.C." I'd called her Mrs. O'Connell only once. She preferred M.C.

Hanging from the walker was a basket lined with fake brown fur. Home to Kitty, a nearly bald ten-thousand-year-old apricot poodle (yes, Kitty is a dog) who couldn't walk. When I leaned over to scratch her head, she growled and bared the few yellow teeth she had left. I pulled back. Not from fear, but because the smell from the dog's mouth made me queasy.

"'Bout time," M.C. complained. "I called Friday, and they weren't ready."

"Friday was nuts," I said. Three-quarters of the customers at Bartell's were lonely seniors. I liked talking to them as long as they didn't bring up bodily functions.

"Your hair's growing in nice." Like Kitty, M.C. was nearly bald. She obviously missed having hair, because she always commented on mine.

"Yeah." Six months ago, I hacked off my long blond hair. After Logan died, kids I didn't even know started coming up and asking if I was "the girlfriend of the dead guy." My friends kept telling me I was different too. I didn't need the judgment or the attention. But instead of flying under the radar, I decided to *be* different. So I hacked off my hair. It was a dumb thing to do.

"The color looks nice."

It was blond, the same color it had always been. "I'm thinking of dying it midnight black next month." I played with Logan's St. Christopher medallion. I'd been wearing it since the accident. "To mark—" I stopped.

The one-year anniversary.

Everybody kept telling me I had to get over Logan; I had to move on. Like I could get *over* him. And anyway, my sadness kept him close. My sadness and his medallion—they were the only things I had left. "To mark Halloween," I lied.

M.C. sniffed. "All Hallows' Eve is about more than black hair and broomsticks. It's a true pagan holiday." Her pale blue eyes took on a sudden gleam as she leaned close. "It's the time of year that spirits can most easily make contact with the living." She frowned at the look on my face. "It's true!" She grabbed my arm. "I talk to my Danny boy every year at midnight. You can talk to your Logan too."

I didn't want to talk to Logan. Getting in that car was the stupidest thing he'd ever done. The shock of his death had worn off, and I didn't cry every day anymore, but I hadn't forgiven him or me or Tom. Especially not Tom. He'd bought the beer. And insisted they race.

When I didn't answer, M.C. dropped my arm in disgust. "Okay, so you're a nonbeliever."

The truth was, I believed the dead go somewhere. It's not just lights-out, erased forever like a mistake on a test. That wouldn't be logical. In nature, everything gets recycled. Why should we be any different?

"I know you Christians." M.C. stared at Logan's St. Christopher medallion. "You've been fed a load of bull crap about All Hallows' Eve. I'm telling you, it's about as far from the devil as a daffodil."

You Christians. I thought of my friend Marie. "I'm not sure I'm Christian, M.C."

"What are you then?"

"Undecided." And before she could demand more, I changed the subject. "You'd better go get those pills before Bentley goes on his break."

"Undecided is for wusses and politicians," M.C. said as she headed for the door. "Smart people believe in something."

I walked across the parking lot to the grass on the corner. I believed in lots of things. Tennis and lululemon yoga pants. The importance of saving. Love. And God too, in a casual go-to-church-at-Christmas kind of way.

Later, after it happened, I wondered if being a go-to-church-every-Sunday kind of girl would have spared me. Then again, it might have made it worse.

I flung myself on the grass between two clumps of flowers—one orange with brown centers, the other a brilliant pink—and wedged my pop on the ground beside me. Once, this spot had been nothing but bark mulch and a few droopy shrubs. You could still see it in old pictures showing our location. But last year Bentley had removed the bark mulch, laid sod and thrown down a fistful of wildflower seeds.

For a guy who dealt drugs all day, he sure liked his flowers. Especially ones that smelled good.

The sun beat on my face. I settled with a sigh. The odd car drove up and down the street. Geese honked somewhere above me. Relaxed and finally warm, I shut my eyes.

I drifted, thinking of homework, of foods class. We'd been assigned groups to prepare theme dinners. I'd been set up with Tom, who insisted we choose Mexican because he wanted to cook with tequila. Like that would fly. Still, knowing Tom, he'd find a way to screw the rules, and we'd fail.

Tom brought thoughts of Logan.

Who was I kidding? Whenever I shut my eyes, I almost always thought of Logan.

Except, I was starting to forget the way he smelled. Don't be grossed out. Logan smelled better than anyone I'd ever known. I'd even bought a bottle of his cologne to wear. But it didn't smell the same on me as it did on him. Body chemistry, I guess.

Forcing myself to think of something else, I concentrated on the roll of earth at the small of my back, the scratch of grass beneath my palms, the warmth of the sun on my eyelids.

I floated there for a while, knowing it was almost time to go back inside. Just as I was about to sit up, I heard a slight buzz in my ear, felt a soft tickle on my cheek. I imagined it was Logan teasing me with a blade of grass. I imagined what I would do back and grew hotter still. The buzz faded; the tickling dropped to my chin.

Some kind of bug. I brushed at my face, heard an angry buzz, and then I felt it—a sharp sting on my neck.

"Ow!" The pain was intense, red-hot and scorching.

A bee sting. My first.

It had to happen sometime. And what better place to get stung than outside a drug store where I knew the pharmacist and he could pull the lid on a bottle of Calamine lotion without me paying for it.

I grabbed my soda and scrambled to my feet. Sunlight glinted off the cars passing by, the sky was an unreal pencil-crayon blue. A car horn sounded; a child laughed. The noises rushed in, filled me up.

Probably I should get the stinger out, I thought. Weren't you supposed to?

A wave of dizziness turned the world sideways. Nerves, I told myself. It was only a bee sting. No biggie.

Except the pain was spreading. Down my neck and into my chest. Sweat beaded my forehead.

Don't be silly. You're going to be fine.

I hurried toward the parking lot. The dizziness was getting worse, the noise from the cars growing louder. I knew about shock reactions; I'd learned something working at Bartell's for the last eight months. But no one in my family was allergic. To anything.

By the time I got to the parking lot, I knew I was wrong. Someone in our family was allergic to something. And that someone was me. My legs felt like they were going uphill through cement. My arms tingled, my breath was wooly in my throat.

Across the lot, I saw M.C. and her stupid Kitty dog standing in the doorway talking to Lila.

I started to run. And then everything turned black.